Arthur Gordon Burgoyne, Frederick Earl Johnston

Shakespeare Up to Date

And Other Latter-day Lyrics

Arthur Gordon Burgoyne, Frederick Earl Johnston

Shakespeare Up to Date
And Other Latter-day Lyrics

ISBN/EAN: 9783744796996

Printed in Europe, USA, Canada, Australia, Japan

Cover: Foto ©Andreas Hilbeck / pixelio.de

More available books at **www.hansebooks.com**

SHAKESPEARE ✳

✳ UP TO DATE

—AND—

OTHER LATTER-DAY LYRICS

—BY—

Arthur G. Burgoyne,

("All Sorts" Man of the Pittsburg
"Leader").

Illustrated by
FREDERICK EARL JOHNSTON.

T. W. Nevin, Publisher,
Pittsburg, Pa.
1896.

INTRODUCTORY.

The verses collected in this little volume are offered to the public as an example of rough-and-ready newspaper jingle, literally "dashed off" by the writer as a part of his daily allotment of labor.

Every day since October 13, 1890, the "All Sorts" column of the Pittsburg "Leader" has been headed with a bit of verse, dealing with the leading topic of the hour, or, in case the leading topic happened to be stale or unpalatable, with some more congenial theme, arbitrarily chosen. As a rule, however, the metrical department held its own as a department of current comment and moved along "pari passu" with the editorial column.

Of course, there could be no polishing of these "lyrics" under the circumstances governing their manufacture. The poetical machinery worked at high pressure and the period of production was usually from five to thirty minutes.

Nevertheless the writer, having been

bred in a school of literary effort which knows not fear or trembling, submits the accompanying gems to the great world outside the sphere of the "Leader" with a cheerful indifference to the consequences.

If any man's life should be brightened or his home broken up by these machine-made verses, the author will still be honest enough to confess that they were not, like the works of most other metrical performers of modern times, written with a "purpose." It is merely as a specimen of mechanical art, operating under a full head of steam, that they are submitted by

THE AUTHOR.

RICHARD III.

Of subjects dramatic there's none more
    absurd
Than that bull-headed Englishman Rich-
    ard the Third,
For although he was wealthy and sat on
    a throne
He could never let first degree murder
    alone.

Old Shakespeare veraciously tells us that
    Dick
(So we'll call him for short) had an im-
    becile trick
Of arousing his relatives out of their beds
And exclaiming excitedly, "Orf with their
    'eds!"

As a bracer each morning he'd string up
    a lord;
As a nightcap, a duke he would put to the
    sword;
When he'd bowl up on sack—very prime
    was his stock—
A round dozen of viscounts he'd send to
    the block.

Two juvenile nephews he lodg'd in the
    Tow'r,
Where the poor little chaps were cut off
    in their flow'r;
Brother Clarence, who tippled, he brought
    into line
By submerging the sot in a hogshead of
    wine.

He surprised Rivers, Buckingham, Hast-
    ings and Gray
By abruptly removing their craniums one
    day,
And, though hunchbacked and cock-eyed
    and evil of tongue,
He attempted to copy the late Brigham
    Young.

While his record of felonies always was
    full,
The courts wouldn't try him because of
    his "pull,"
And if anyone threatened to cure him by
    force
He'd advance to the footlights and swear
    he'd do worse.

The people of England knew well he did
    wrong,
But had no secret ballot to help them
    along;
"What's the use of reform," they de-
    jectedly said,
"When the high moral hustler must part
    with his head?"

But at last Colonel Richmond, a gallant
    free lance,
Who had long found it healthy to linger
    in France,
Recruited an army, resolved on a kick,
And declared, by the gods, that he'd wal-
    lop King Dick.

At Bosworth they met—'twas a place
    apropos—
For King Dick was a Boss worth defeat-
    ing, you know.
There his liver went wrong on the eve
    of the fight
And a horrible dream made him squirm
    all the night.

The ghosts of his victims emerged from
the tomb
And appeared in his tent with predictions
of gloom.
The calcium burnt blue as each muttered
a curse,
And the king woke up raving and called
for a horse.

The battle came off and King Dick lost
his life,
While Richmond triumphantly ended the
strife.
Then the victor stepped front with the
crown on his brow,
And the gallery gods raised a deuce of a
row.

7

HAMLET.

There lived in Denmark years ago
  A princeling adolescent,
Who always was in spirits low,
  And never could be pleasant.
His stockings were of solemn black;
  His cloak was made of camlet;
His stock of names was very slack—
  'Twas limited to "Hamlet."

His family disgraced the town;
  The most of 'em were crooked;
His father wore a nobby crown;
  His uncle schemed to hook it.
A dose of poison did the act,
  ('Twas given circumspectly.)
The uncle by the queen was backed
  And married her directly.

The specter of the king appeared
  And said in tones appalling:
"O Ham, my son, your dad revered,
  Though dead, for gore is calling.
Your uncle is a scalawag,
  Your mother is no better;
Just kill 'em both—pray, do not lag—
  And I will be your debtor."

At this poor Ham went off his nut,
  And in his awful hurry
Polonius to death he cut,
  Thus adding to his worry.
Polonius was Ham's girl's papa
  And—O! the torture scathing!—
The girl went mad—yes, mad, ha! ha!
  And drowned herself while bathing.

Then came Polonius' only son
  Laertes, like a lion,
He went for Hamlet with a gun
  And thought to leave him dyin';
With poison and a fencing foil
  He tried the Prince to slaughter,
But Ham knew how his game to spoil
  And killed him as he oughter.

The king and queen by accident
  Drank Hamlet's poisoned chalice.
Then Ham took one himself; he meant
  To show he bore no malice.
As all the family now were dead
  Through circumstances squally,
Old Shakespeare, with a level head,
  Here wrote the word "Finale."

SHYLOCK.

In a period archaic
  Dwelt in Venice by the sea
An old gentleman Hebraic
  Just as stingy as could be.
Ev'ry one that saw his sly look
  When a ducat hove in view,
Would exclaim, "That Mr. Shylock
  Is a skinflint through and through."

Sweet Miss Portia was an heiress
  With a goodly store of pelf;
And besides she was as fair as—
  Well, as fair as Love itself.
And her beaux she loved to baffle,
  Young Bassanio 'mid the rest;
But he won her at a raffle
  And he pressed her to his vest.

While Bassanio fixed his fences,
  He was nicely kept afloat,
For Antonio paid expenses
  With a promissory note.
Shylock cashed it; Bass securing
  The proceeds, said, "Israelite
When this notelet is maturing
  You may walk the floor all night."

The security provided
  By Antonio was a pound
Of his flesh, if he backslided
  When the settling time came round.
As he didn't have a copper
  Shylock swore he was a "beat,"
And with expletives improper,
  Vowed he'd have his pound of meat.

Poor Antonio was arrested
  And was brought before the Duke
To be legally invested
  With the status of a crook.
But the news abroad did journey
  And when Portia heard the tale
She dressed up as an attorney
  And got Tony out on bail.

At the trial, Purdon's digest
  She produced and in the same
Found the groundwork for a sly jest—
  'Twas a clever little game.
"Mr. Shylock," she said sweetly,
  "With your little butcher knife
Cut an even pound off neatly
  Or the law will have your life."

Shylock wilted; there was no test;
  Portia won by iron gall;
And the note—it went to protest
  And was never paid at all.
Not a moment, then, they tarried
  But the bells began to chime,
And they everyone got married
  And had quite a nobby time.

11

JULIUS CAESAR.

In ancient Rome on a street unknown,
　At a number not recorded
A political sharp, of the highest tone,
　With his family lodged and boarded.
　　　　Like Chris Magee
　　　　A boss was he
And historians all agree, sir,
　　　　That in levelness of head
　　　　The universe he led,
Which his name 'twas Julius Caesar.

He went to war with a great hurrah
　And burned his boats behind him,
Wherever the face of an enemy he saw
　In the front you'd always find him.
　　　　The foreigners that kicked
　　　　Were summarily licked
And compelled for their lives to flee, sir,
　　　　And savage folk
　　　　Had to walk 'neath the yoke
Of Commander Julius Caesar.

All Rome turned out with joy to greet
The warrior home returning;
But a few who couldn't with him compete
With envious rage were burning.
They chewed their nails,
Told trumped-up tales,
And were mad as mad could be, sir,
When they saw that all
Were ready to fall
At the feet of Julius Caesar.

Old Brutus, he was the General's chum
And Cassius was another,
While Casca swore that, whate'er might
come,
He loved him as a brother.
As they loved him so,
In their overflow
Of affection true, these three, sir,
Fixed an early date
To assassinate
Ambitious Julius Caesar.

When Julius sought to wear a crown,
The plotters cried, "Have at you,"
Then carved him up and he dropped right
down
At the base of Pompey's statue.
Antonius spake
At the General's wake,
While the tears came fast and free, sir,
And the murderers fled,
Their hands still red,
With the gore of Julius Caesar.

Now Brutus, backed by Cassius, tried
In war to find salvation.
They failed and took to suicide
As a final consolation.
To record their shame
The task became
Of the Stratford bard and he, sir,
Still evokes applause
And the public draws
With the tale of Julius Caesar.

13

OTHELLO.

Shakespeare tells of one Othello,
  An unpleasant sort of fellow,
Who resided once in Venice and enjoyed a
      hefty pull;
  He was black as coal and boorish,
  And his family was Moorish,
Yet an army he commanded and of honors
      he was full.

  Ne'er in Venice was there known a
  Fairer lass than Desdemona—
She was spooney on Othello, and the pair
      of 'em eloped;
  Old Bassanio, her father,
  Swore by all the gods he'd rather
Have been ruined than to see her into such
      a marriage roped.

  On the foul miscegenation
  People frowned disapprobation,
And Othello was hauled up before the sign-
      iors, grave and wise.
  "You're a black," said they, indignant.
  "She's a beaut," said he, benignant.
And the signiors dropped the case when
      thus he did apologize.

Of Othello's guards the highest
One was Cassio, and the slyest
Was Iago, who was jealous of the Moor
    and Cassio, too.
Now this cunning basilisk, he
Got young Cassio full of whisky,
Whereupon Othello bounced the youth, as
    duty bade him do.

Desdemona interceded
For the victim, and she pleaded
So devoutly that Iago saw his chance to
    play the deuce.
"See, Othello," said the villain,
"Cassio loves her and she's willin'
With that whisky-drinking scalawag to
    play you fast and loose."

Then a handkerchief was flashed up
Which the Moor completely smashed
    up
Since Iago said that Desdemona gave it to
    her beau.
Says Othello: "Talk is idle,
Nothing short of homicidal
Demonstrations will content me in the case
    of Mrs. O."

Thereupon he wildly snorted,
And with visage much distorted,
Sword in hand he sought the chamber
    where sweet Desdemona slept.
But too sweet she was for stabbing,
So thought he: "I'll do no jabbing;
It might hurt the girl," and at the thought
    he sat him down and wept.

Finally, his nerve regaining,
He could brook no more restraining,
So he seized the sofa pillow and with that
    he did the deed.
As they nevermore could wake her,
To bring in an undertaker
Was the next thing on the program in this
    mournful hour of need.

On the instant, loud lamenting,
Came Iago's wife, repenting
That she hadn't spoken out before, since
    now it was too late.
Out of fear she had suppressed it,
But she freely now confessed it,
That Iago had been lying and that Mrs. O.
    was straight.

When he heard this sad recital
Then Othello pierced a vital
Portion of his composition with his jewel-
    hilted blade.
Thus the circus terminated
And the audience much elated
O'er the wind-up, thought a sweeter play
    than this was never made.

TIMON OF ATHENS.

See, on this figure appears the stamp,
  The thorough, indelible brand,
Which characterizes the genus tramp,
The chap who, whether 'tis dry or damp,
  Goes strolling about the land.
Free lunch and of rum an occasional
      drain
He chases, but labor is in vain,
  He'd have you understand.

Our sample was the first of his race;
  In Athens he used to dwell.
Lord Timon he was till he sank from
      grace;
For the gilded youth he set the pace
  And was counted a howling swell.
With lavish hand his cash he spent,
And with lightning speed to the bow-
      wows went
  And into the gutter fell.

The Coal Oil Johnny of Greece was he
  And parasites hemmed him round;
Lucullus, Sempronius and Lucius were
    three
That "pulled his leg." He was soft, you
    see,
  And 'twas thus that he ran aground.
For the fellow that scatters his ready
    cash
On ev'ry hand in a manner rash
  To go by the board is bound.

Collectors thronged at his palace door;
  His notes to protest went;
Of letters he got full many a score
The legend "please remit" they bore;
  And his landlord sued for rent.
He tried to borrow from friends es-
    teemed,
But wofully short of cash they seemed;
  They'd lend him nary a cent.

At this Lord Timon's rage was great,
  And his curses rent the air.
He cursed the city; he cursed the state;
And then he fled on a passing freight,
  For he had no railroad fare.
Quoth he, "Humanity's all a cheat
Henceforth I'll be nought but a stone-
    dead beat
  And cast-off clothes I'll wear."

Thus Timon laid the foundation stone
  Of trampdom, and to-day
The Knights of the Road, who make
    their moan
At kitchen doors in a puling tone,
  Their homage are bound to pay
To the memory of their prototype,
Whose rags and bundle and short clay
    pipe
  Are the "motif" of Shakespeare's play.

17

THE COMEDY OF ERRORS.

There were four twins—two pair, you
    know,
  A set of real jolly cusses;
And two were known as Dromio
  And two of 'em were Antipholuses.

Will Shakespeare picked these duplex
    twins,
  Foredoom'd to strange mishaps and
    terrors,
To move the world to broadest grins
  Throughout a "Comedy of Errors."

Each Dromio with an Antipholus
  As body-servitor abided.
The one pair lived at Ephesus,
  The other at Syracuse resided.

A shipwreck split the pairs apart
  In infancy, but human "natur"
Inspired them, with a loving heart,
  To try and see each other later.

So, years thereafter, o'er the sea,
  Supplied with information scanty,
Went "Anti" Number One. Thought he,
  "Perchance I'll find the other 'Anti.' "

His dad, Aegeon, paid his fare,
  And went along, his bosom thawing
As he beheld one "Anti" there
  And hoped two pair he might be draw-
    ing.

Arrived at Ephesus, they found
  That four of a kind knocks two pair
    silly;
All four were mixed and twisted round,
  And things began to turn out illy.

The wife of "Anti" Number Two
  Took Number One for hers and slapped
    him,
While Number Two, by men in blue
  Was gobbled, who in prison clapped
    him.

The Dromios, too, were more or less
  Confounded, railed at, kicked and sat
    on.
In short both pairs, we must confess,
  Were bad to draw to, or else stand pat
    on.

To make things worse Aegeon was jailed
  And doomed to death without rhyme
    or reason;
And being in durance, of course he failed
  To open the jack-pot in proper season.

But just at the time when 'twas agreed
  That all hands round were drunk or
    crazy,
Aegeon, en route to the gallows, took
    heed
  Of the several twins and the happ'nings
    mazy.

By strawberry marks, 'twas all made
    straight
  And the twins reuned in a style de-
    voted.
Aegeon was freed at an early date
  And a royal flush on his cheek was
    noted.

Then a long-lost mother came on the
    scene
  And greeted the crowd with embraces
    hearty;
Whereat all hands, with emotion keen,
  Cashed in their chips and broke up the
    party.

19

MRS. MACBETH.

Do not tell us of Susan B. Anthony's
    fame
  Or of sweet Lillie Devereux Blake;
Do not tell us that these in the woman's
    rights game
  Take the laurel, the palm and the cake.
For we've looked up the records and find
    'tis a fact
  (So Shakespeare decisively saith);
That there's none that can beat in the
    masculine act
  Her Scotch ladyship, Mrs. Macbeth.
    for life

When she made her debut she was mated
  To the cousin of Duncan, the king;
And she said to herself, "To be royalty's
    wife
  Would be quite an agreeable thing."
So she argued with Mac that by hook or
    by crook
  He was bound to put Duncan to death,
And his nerve fled away 'neath the
    basilisk look
  Fastened on him by Mrs. Macbeth.

King Duncan to visit Macbeth was in-
duced,
And he took Captain Banquo along.
"Ah ha!" said the lady, aside, "You'll be
goosed,
Unless matters with Mac should go
wrong."
As for Mac, he met witches, who led him
astray,
And by ghosts he was robbed of his
breath.
Even daggers intangible rose in his way—
He'd have quit but for Mrs. Macbeth.

Egged on by the woman, the man did the
deed,
And Duncan was slain in his sleep;
Next Banquo was killed, and from rivalry
freed,
Mac arrived at the top of the heap.
But his conscience rebuked him; strange
visions he saw;
Of each victim there bobbed up the
wraith.
Still whenever he took to lamenting; "Oh,
pshaw,"
Was the answer of Mrs. Macbeth.

At last from the furthest recesses of
Fife
Came Macduff with a force of his own;
Put an end to Macbeth, after murderous
strife,
And gave Malcolm the use of the throne.
Thus fell the conspirators, e'en though
they got
From the witches a queer shibboleth;
And, from that day to this, there is cer-
tainly not
Any rival to Mrs. Macbeth.

FALSTAFF.

Before the days of anti-fat
  There lived a doughty knight,
A sort of walking liquor vat,
  Who ev'ry day got tight.
He guzzled sack at such a pace,
  To stop he knew not when;
It took a mile of belt to brace
  His knightly abdomen.

His name was Falstaff and the same
  His nature did express;
For false stuff, never feeling shame,
  He dealt in to excess.
He was the greatest fakir that
  Great Britain e'er produced,
And never cared where he was at
  When once his tongue was loosed.

The knight was fond of ladies fair;
  A gay Lothario he.
He went to Windsor once and there
  With matrons two made free.
Fair Mistress Page and Mistress Ford
  Enchained the rascal's gaze.
He vowed to each that he adored
  Her charms and winning ways.

These "Merry Wives of Windsor" laid
  A trap to catch the knight.
A false pretense of love they made
  Which fooled the luckless wight.
They made him in a basket hide
  From those who came to seek;
And when he once was fast inside
  They threw him in the creek.

Again they lured him on and dressed
  The knight in woman's clothes.
Witch hunters chased him then with
    zest
  And multiplied his woes.
His carcass fat they kicked and cuffed,
  Belabored, smacked and switched.
Says Falstaff, "I'm a Prophet stuffed
  Like Cleveland, or bewitched."

And once at night those matrons twain
  Enticed him to a dell,
Where goblins tried, with might and
    main,
  His am'rous mood to quell.
They pinched his flesh and burned his
    toes
  And pulled his scanty hair.
Says Falstaff, "That's enough; here
    goes;
  I'll try a change of air."

To London fast himself he hied
  And bottled sack consumed,
Until of Keeley cure he died
  And fitly was entombed.
To fat men Falstaff's life should be
  A warning to refrain
From rum and wenches, which, you see,
  Upset this fat man's brain.

ANTONY AND CLEOPATRA.

Antony he was a Roman bold,
With a handsome face and a heap of
    gold.
When Brutus and Cassius to pieces went,
To rule over Asia he was sent.
And there, at Tarsus, one day he met
A widow whose charms he could ne'er
    forget.
Mrs. Cleopatra—that was her name;
And to capture a beau was her little
    game.

Refrain.

See Antonius gazing on her lovely face,
Pouring forth his sentiments with ease
    and grace;
Not another suitor could get in the race,
  They fitted one another like a glove.
"Come with me to Egypt, 'honeybird,"
    says she;
"Certainly," says Antony, "I'll stick to
    thee."
When from duty fellows thus inanely
    flee,
    That is love; that is love.

At Alexandria Antony stayed
For numerous moons with the lovesick
maid.
She was a queen, and of long green stuff
For all expenses had quite enough.
Adown the Cydnus in boats they sailed,
And with hugs and kisses themselves re-
galed,
Till a telegraph message arrived from
Rome,
Which summoned the amorous Antony
home.

Refrain.

See Antonius weeping as his bark he
steers
Far away from Cleopatra, bathed in
tears;
That he never may return the widow
fears;
She is like a tender stricken dove.
"Antony, my petlet," o'er the brine she
cries;
"Come back soon again and live in para-
dise."
Twenty miles away he heard her sobs
and sighs—
That is love; that is love.

Octavius Caesar was now the boss
In Rome, and when Antony came across
"A truce to your monkey work," he said;
"My sister Octavia you shall wed."
The wedding took place, and the bridal
pair
To Asia went for change of air;
But Antony, tired of wedded life,
Went back to Egypt and shook his wife.

Refrain.

See Antonius meet again his beauteous
queen.
Widows are his weakness; that is plainly
seen.
"Mark you, Cleopatra," he remarks, "I've
been
Forced for you my wife aside to shove."
"What of that, my love?" the lady softly
coos,
"Don't let little things like that give you
the blues,
For when people don't know which's wife
is whose,
That is love; that is love."

Young Octavius came over the sea;
He whipped Antonius and made him flee.
Antonius thought he had been betrayed
By Cleopatra, and so he made
A skillful attempt at suicide,
And then in the lady's arms he died.
Here the widow's heart in anguish
    breaks,
And she dies of a genuine case of snakes.

Refrain.

See Antonius done up; Cleopatra, too;
See the flow'rs wherewith kind friends
    their grave bestrew;
See the legend on a tombstone, fair to
    view,
    "Both Of 'Em (perhaps) Have Gone
    Above."
People think, "Well, well, it doesn't seem
    to pay
When a married gentleman becomes too
    gay."
But the sentimental ones drop tears and
    say,
    "That is love; that is love."

HISTORICAL

AND

POLITICAL.

27

ELECTION DAY.

Daybreak: The dawn with smiling face
Illuminates the polling place;
Lights up the frosty sidewalk where
Election officers repair,
To figure out with caution due
Which one is which and who is who,
And, swearing one another in,
The business of the day begin.
Inspectors, clerks and judges, all
Within the booths themselves install;
And watchers, early on the ground,
Look wise and idly stand around
Till with a self-approving grin,
The first stray voter ambles in.
A candidate or two comes by
To see that nothing is awry,
And in the foreground, full of grace,
A copper stands and twirls his mace.

Midday: Now doth the fight wax hot,
A hundred men are on the spot;
The heeler, rounder, thug and bloat
Beset ,the man who wants to vote.
In all 'directions, left and right,
Police and firemen are in sight,
With hosts of other active chaps,
Who live on soft official snaps.
The challenger now cuts a swath
And leaves his victims white with wrath.
Prone in the dust will he be laid
Whose taxes yet remain unpaid.
The candidates, with anxious air,
Are here and there and ev'rywhere;
Liquor there is in large supply;
From hand to hand the greenbacks fly,
While calm and heedless of the fray
The Baker ballot pounds away.

Evening: The hard-fought battle's o'er,
The warriors cleansed themselves of
        gore.
Still on the sidewalk loafs the crowd,
Beery, obstreperous and loud.
The board within takes off its coat,
And figures up the total vote.
At last returns are given out,
And greeted with a rousing shout.
Moved by the mob's approving cheers,
The winners set up countless beers.
The losers, when they hear the news,
Sneak off unseen and get the blues.
This ends it all. At once the town
Gets sobered up and simmers down;
Business resumes its even flow,
All things return to statu quo,
And war's alarms are filed away
Until the next election day.

JIM BLAINE.

"Blaine, Blaine!"—No more that cry shall
    be
In chorus raised from sea to sea
        With jubilation.
For just as victory's jeweled crown
Was in his grasp, our Jim backs down,
        And scares the nation.

Republicans on bended knees
Entreated Jimmy—Would he please
        Be standard bearer?
A unit in his cause they stood,
And swore that thus they'd stay; what
    could
        Than this be fairer?

Long like a sort of modern sphinx,
Jim held his peace, as though, methinks,
        The prospect liking,
Those states that boast of fav'rite sons
Felt positive that soon their guns
        He would be spiking.

30

B. Harrison with steps infirm
Marched feebly on, a second term
    In office seeking,
While others, in the background hid,
Made for B. H.'s shoes a bid,
    Reserved and sneaking.

But just as long as Blaine kept mum
And people thought he'd forward come
    At any minute,
Those other chaps of minor note
Could bank on not a single vote—
    They were not in it.

Hence are we stricken with surprise
While, unrestricted, from our eyes
    Hot tears are welling,
To hear that Blaine's resolved at last
The people's gift aside to cast,
    High hopes dispelling.

Thus does the cruel hand of fate
Leave Quay without a candidate;
    He's one of many
Who, if for Blaine they cannot vote,
Won't climb into the selfsame boat
    With little Benny.

Where are we now to take our stand,
With scores of lesser lights on hand
    To claim succession?
Alger and Sherman, Cullom, Reed
And Bill McKinley seek to lead
    The big procession.

But stifled is the public voice;
We're powerless now to make a choice,—
    That's how we view it—
Since we're forever robbed of him
Whose cinch was ironclad—Confound you,
    Jim,
        Why did you do it?

GROVER'S BEACON.

There stands 'way up north, on a wave-
 beaten coast,
 A cottage, old-fashioned and gray,
That defies the wild Storm King's infuriate
 host,
 Sweeping nightly across Buzzards Bay.
There a babe and its mother in solitude
 sleep,
 Far away from the object they love,
While with touching devotion they fail
 not to keep
A light in the window for Grove.

Refrain.

Far, far away
From the statesman they ardently love,
Until after election
They'll keep with affection
A light in the window for Grove.

If Grove is elected, that candle will be
  To the White house transferred the next
    day,
And whene'er the old man knocks around
  in D. C.,
  To his home it will lighten the way.
Mrs. C. may be mad and Miss Ruth be in
  tears
  When the boss arrives, chewing a clove,
But there's one thing that never will fall
  in arrears—
  That light in the window for Grove.

     Refrain.—Far, far away, etc.

If Grove is defeated, in sorrow he'll slink
  Buzzards bayward, to drop out of sight.
Such a backset would drive weaker spirits
  to drink,
  Or at least to get partially tight.
But there still will be one thing to lighten
  the blow,
  Though misfortunes flock round in a
    drove;
'Tis that blessed, unchanging, affectionate
  glow
  Of the light in the window for Grove.

     Refrain.—Far, far away, etc.

So cheer up, Mrs. C., don't be gloomy of
  soul.
  What's the odds if your hubby is
    whipped?
He's hardly entitled to kick, on the whole,
  If by Ben in the race he's outstripped.
You and Ruth can console him in chill
  winter nights,
  When you're all huddled up round the
    stove,
By recalling the one thing wherein he de-
  lights—
  That light in the window for Grove.

     Refrain.—Far, far away, etc.

QUEEN LIL.

With teardrops in her lovely eyes,
  The Sandwich Lily came
      To Grover,
      Good old Grover.
To reassume her queenly guise
  She sweetly filed a claim
      With Grover,
      Good old Grover.
Says she, "Oh, Mr. President, you're chiv-
  alrous, I know;
You would not be a party to a lady's over-
  throw,
And hence for restoration quite confiding-
  ly I go
      To Grover,
      Good old Grover."

Her skin as dark as Erebus,
Her air of regal grace
Caught Grover,
Good old Grover.
"I'm happy, madam, to discuss
Your interesting case,"
Quoth Grover,
Good old Grover.
"Your dusky kind of beauty has its own
peculiar charm
That moves me to relieve you from the
slightest dread of harm.
If any one is competent your foemen to
disarm,
It's Grover,
Good old Grover."

He summoned then the cabinet,
Which held a grave pow-wow
With Grover,
Good old Grover.
They said, "We'll help the lady yet
And set her right somehow   .
Through Grover,
Good old Grover.
The age of chivalry endures; on that it's
safe. to bank;
And since some scamps have ventured
Lily's crown away to yank,
Who is there in the universe that can re-
store her rank
But Grover,
Good old Grover?"

The smoothest goldsmith in the town
Was summoned, and he came
To Grover,
Good old Grover.
"Oh, make me quick a golden crown
With jewels in the same,"
Said Grover,
Good old Grover.
The crown was made; no monarch could
a finer head-dress wear;
Instanter it was placed upon the Lily's
kinky hair,
And now the greatest man on earth, Ha-
waiians all declare,
Is Grover,
Good old Grover.

35

THE CZAR.

The Czar prowls around with a crown on
    his head
   And jewels bedecking his clothes,
While his subjects around him are howling
      for bread
   Which to give them he doesn't propose.
Small wonder that bombshells are thrown
      with a view
   His royal appearance to mar,
And that people should ask, as they fre-
      quently do,
   What on earth is the use of the Czar?

He has prying policemen, who revel in
      fees,
   Contingent on ev'ry arrest,·
Oligarchic marauders who do as they
      please,
   And do it with merciless zest.
Though you're guiltless of crime, they'll
      arrest you on sight,
   And send you to prison afar,
In Siberia's wastes, where you'll think day
   ⌄ and night
   What on earth is the use of the Czar?

Petowsky gets banished for winking his
    eye,
  Petoffsky because of his looks,
Poniwisky because he's indulged in a sigh,
  And Kawoski for fooling with books.
And so many male Owskys and Offskys
    are fired,
  That, as if by the fortune of war,
Farms are turned into deserts, and then
    'tis inquired
  What on earth is the use of the Czar?

The Hebrews in Russia are hard-working
    souls,
  With a habit of saving their cash.
"Drive them out!" roars the Czar, who has
    had a few bowls,
  "Drive them out, or I'll do something
    rash."
So out they are driven with curses and
    jeers
  And many an infamous scar.
Yes, indeed, 'tis a question to puzzle the
    seers:
  What on earth is the use of the Czar?

Our government's sending a shipload of
    grain
  To Russia, the poor to relieve;
And a chance now we'll have that may
    not come again
  A righteous exploit to achieve.
Man the vessel with mariners powerful
    of lung,
  And instruct every jolly Jack Tar,
That on landing the chorus sublime must
    be sung:
  What on earth is the use of the Czar?

THE SILVERITES.

Listen to the never ending chin,
       Silver chin.
What a world of prosy yarns the toga-
    wearers spin,
  As they gabble, gabble, gabble
   Every morning, noon and night,
  Like some idiotic rabble
  That goes in for idle babble
   With unlimited delight,
  Prosing on, on, on,
  Never, never to get done.
And for popular opinion they seem not to
    care a pin,
As they chin, chin, chin, chin, chin, chin,
    chin,
As they wantonly and garrulously chin.

Hear the voice of Stewart—he's a bore,
       Ancient bore.
Every day you're sure to find him spouting
    on the floor.
  How he proses, proses, proses,
   Quoting figures by the yard,
  And outlandish schemes proposes,
   Which his colleagues must discard!
  He is slick, slick, slick,

And to silver he will stick,
Till the surface of gehenna ultimately
   freezes o'er.
He's a bore, bore, bore, bore, bore, bore,
   bore,
An obnoxious and insufferable bore.

Peffer, too, inanely blows his horn,
            Silver horn.
In the side of level headed people he's a
   thorn.
   He keeps quoting, quoting, quoting
      From innumeiable books,
   And repeaters bent on voting
      Find they can't get in their hooks,
   For old Peff, Peff, Peff
   To all arguments is deaf,
And his hearers w.sh he never (here's
   where Peff is met with scorn)
Had been born, born, born, born, born,
   born, born,
'Tis a pity that old Peff was ever born.

Cameron and Allen have their say,
            Stupid say.
But they cannot capture such a bright old
   bird as Quay.
   Though they're swearing, swearing,
      swearing,
      That free coinage can't be downed,
   Matthew Stanley isn't caring,
      And with firmness holds his ground,
   Saying, "Don, Don, Don,
   All your prestige now is gone,
Having thrown your party loyalty un-
   blushingly away,
You're too gay, gay, gay, gay, gay, gay
   gay,
For the Keystone state, old chap, you are
   too gay."

What's the use of wasting time in fur-
   ther chat,
            Idle chat?
How can we find out where we financially
   are at
   If in talking, talking, talking,
      All the senate's time is spent.
   While the nation's hope it's balking
      To a pitiful extent?
   Making breaks, breaks, breaks,
   And nonsensical mistakes.
Yes, the senate does its talking—please to
   make a note of that—
Through its hat, hat, hat, hat, hat, hat,
   hat,
Through its brickbat-lined and humbug-
   cov'ring hat.

            39

THE RACE FOR OFFICE.

Was there ever a queerer district than
    the Twenty-fourth congressional,
  Where you cannot throw a stone but
    what you hit a candidate?
You can see them flocking forward in a
    manner that's processional,
  Defying any citizen to do his voting
    straight.
Oh, it's wonderful the sight that greets
    the visitor that catches on
  To things as there they stand to-day
    and the circumstances probes,
He'll encounter Andy Stewart, Sipe and
    Editor Erny Acheson,
  Together with Johnny Cox and Rev.
    Campbell Set-Up Jobes.

"Can it be," he'll cry in wonder, "that
    these chaps are all petitioners
  For a single seat in congress? Bless
    my soul, it can't be so!"
Yet it doesn't take an inquiry by elec-
    toral commissioners

To find that every man of 'em believes
　　he has a show.
Each keeps hustling like a major and
　　proclaims that he a dandy is,
And ready his antagonists with awful
　　force to swipe;
That's the kind of a ranting, roaring pol-
　　itician Colonel Andy is,
And also Rev. Set-Up Jobes, Cox, Ache-
　　son and Sipe.

In Fayette the folks are furious; in
　　Greene they are uproarious,
And here in Allegheny they are simply
　　raising Cain;
Little Washington is swearing in a style
　　that's quite notorious,
And Homestead vows that Chris and
　　Flinn won't boss the boys again.
Up in Uniontown the hayseed politicians
　　(sly old foxes) say
They'll never support a bolter—they'd
　　prefer to be undone;
And they watch with breathless interest
　　the feats that Sipe and Cox essay,
Together with Colonel Andy, Jobes and
　　Erny Acheson.

Where, oh, where, we'd like to know, is
　　all this rumpus going to terminate?
And who will be the gory-handed victor
　　over which?
When everybody means a heap of rivals
　　to exterminate,
There's sure to be for somebody a mon-
　　umental hitch.
Now, we don't pretend to prophesy, but
　　to state the truth in type is well.
Old Nick himself can't name the winner
　　till the plum he knocks,
But it's certain that there's fun ahead
　　for Set-Up Jobes and Sipe as well,
Together with Colonel Andy,Erny Ache-
　　son and Cox.

41

LI'S DEGRADATION.

PROLOGUE.

Some time ago all China rang
With words of praise for Li Hung Chang,
   The general-in-chief.
He was the Emp'ror's right-hand man,
But in the fracas with Japan,
   Alas, he came to grief.
Because the Emp'ror, tired of chinning,
Had set his royal heart on winning.

ACT I.

Li Hung sent out some sailor chaps
With iron ships to whip the Japs—
   It was a grand array.
But suddenly with furious shout
The Japs came on and knocked 'em out
   And drove those ships away.
Poor Li Hung had to stand the racket,
And lost for this his yellow jacket.

ACT II.

In North Corea, near Ping Yan
The Chinese massed and dared Japan
  To meet them face to face.
At this the Japs got out the ax
And slew those bluffers in their tracks
  To China's great disgrace.
The Emp'ror, rattled altogether,
Now stripp'd off Li Hung's peacock
  feather.

ACT III.

At Pee-Ka-Boo, just as before,
The Japs shed streams of Chinese gore,
  And made the pigtails fly.
They captured drums and guns and stores
And fugitives in scores and scores,
  And this was rough on Li;
For now the Emp'ror, tired of hitches,
Deprived him of his silken breeches.

ACT V.

The Chinamen, to madness stung,
Next hurled their forces at Wun Lung—
  This effort was supreme.
But, as by some magician's art,
The Japs just split those troops apart,
  And spoiled Li's greatest scheme.
Whereat the Emp'ror, filled with loath-
  ing,
Took off Li's costly underclothing.

ACT IV.

Now China tried a hope forlorn,
Which by Japan was laughed to scorn,—
  She knew what was in store.
At Hi-Lo-Jak they met again
And half a million Chinamen
  Went down to rise no more.
This was the last and worst disaster,
And Li Hung lost his porous plaster.

EPILOGUE.

Whene'er the cruel war is o'er
And China quits to fight no more,
  A lesson having learned.
The world will watch with bated breath
To see what treatment worse than death
  Li Hung will then have earned.
Oh, truly, 'twill be base excess
To strip him of his nakedness.

THE MAID OF ORLEANS.

She was young, she was fair,
She had long and wavy hair,
She was gay and free from care
     As a lark,
Till one evening while by chance
She was lying in a trance,
Something said, "Go fight for France,
     Joan of Arc."

At Orleans just then there lay
British troops prepared to slay,
And the dogs of war each day
     Used to bark.
Poor King Charles was yet uncrowned
And he feared he would be downed,
Till the neighbors brought around
     Joan of Arc.

"Bless your majesty," says Joan,
You will soon be on the throne,
Let me play this hand alone"
     (Save the mark!)
"Very well," observed the king,
"Go ahead and have your fling,
But it is a risky thing,
     Joan of Arc."

Soon a charger Joan bestrode,
Wearing armor a la mode,
And of fear the lady showed
　　　Not a spark.
"I'm your general now," said she,
And the army yelled with glee,
For it did 'em good to see
　　　Joan of Arc.

With a sword of monstrous heft,
Joan the foreign army cleft,
And those Britishers were left
　　　Stiff and stark.
Then to Rheims the king she led,
Put the crown upon his head.
"Pray accept this token,", said
　　　Joan of Arc.

Honors great the Maid acquired,
But of quiet growing tired,
Was in war again inspired
　　　To embark.
But the English were her match,
For they managed Joan to catch,
Aye, and hastened to dispatch
　　　Joan of Arc.

Oh, French hearts were like to break
When they burnt her at the stake
As a witch; and hence we make
　　　This remark:
Better far to seek a mate
And enjoy the married state,
Than attempt to emulate
　　　Joan of Arc.

IRISH LOGIC.

Says Patrick O'Casey to Dan Moriarty:
"Och, Dan'l, phat's wrong wid the Dim-
　　mycrat party?
In ould Pennsylvania it used to be hearty,
　　But now, be me sowl, it's disayzed.
There's lashins av bosses that hither and
　　hither
Kape pullin', but bless yez they can't kape
　　togither.
Such eejots the healthiest party wud with-
　　er
　　That iver Americans raised.

"There's Pattison sittin' alone in his
　　glory,
While Wallace an' Harrity shtart in a
　　gory
Death sthruggle, an' Guffey is hammered
　　before he
　　Has time to get into the fuss.
There's Brennen, O'Larey, an' Larkin an'
　　Foley,
　Wid Boyle, that wee gossoon, whose
　　form's roly-poly,
To factional fightin' they're given up
　　wholly.
　　Nice ducks to have pow'r over us."

46

Says Dan Moriarty to Patrick O'Casey,
    "Phy, Pat, sure to answer your ques-
    tion is aisy,
The cause av the scrappin' is not a bit
    hazy,
    'Tis thruth, be the mortial, I sphake.
'Tis the ould Irish blood that is back av
    the rumpus,
An' that pints out the fact at all pints
    av the compass
That clubs among Irishmen always the
    thrump is;
    Now that's what makes Dimmycrats
    wake."

"To the divil," shouts Pat, "wid yer lang-
    widge disgraceful.
"The Irish, ye spalpeen, are dacent an'
    paceful,
Wid holes in a minute I'd fill yer ould
    face full."
    So saying he hits Dan a cuff.
"Arrah, would yez?" says Dan, coming
    back with a soaker,
"If clubs isn't thrumps, phy then here is
    the joker;"
And so they play hob, while some white-
    livered croaker
    Yells "Dimmycrat doctrine's the stuff!"

* * * * * * * * * * * * * *

There's a moral to this that's not hard to
    unravel;
If Democrats would at the enemy cavil
Alone, nor away from that policy travel,
    To make one another eat crow,
They'd be certain to prosper, and oft
    in the battle
By action united the hostiles to rattle
Instead of just butting each other like
    cattle
    And leaving the field to the foe.

47

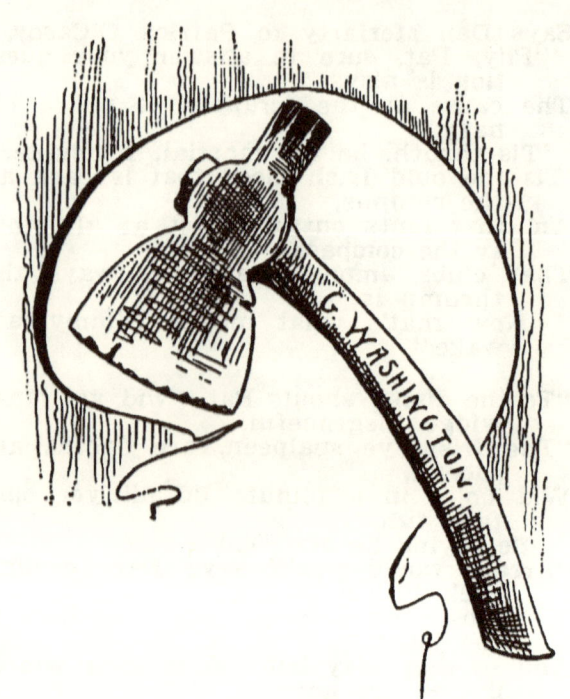

WASHINGTON'S BIRTHDAY.

This is the great and glorious day
When liars in the background stay,
Induced pro tem. themselves to quash
In honor of the late G. Wash,
Who, when his father's plants he'd hack,
Got off on the veracious tack,
And said, with candor in his eye,
"Father, I cannot tell a lie,
E'en though the rod wear out my pants:
'Twas I destroyed your valued plants";
Which frank confession moved his dad
To pardon and reward the lad.

Of course we cannot all come out
Like George in his wood-chopping bout.
For why? Well, that is just because
Our dads are not as George's was.
If valuable trees we chop,
Our governors to think won't stop,
But with a rawhide fell let loose
And lam us like the very deuce;
Whereas, if they'd but grant a stay,
We, too, might try the truthful lay,
Win plaudits by our honest stand,
And check the stern parental hand.

How times have changed since George let
   fly
With active ax and truthful eye!
Degeneracy leaves its trace
On parents well-nigh every place,
And truthful boys, whose dads won't trust,
To lying take in sheer disgust.
Hence comes that awful social pest,
The fakir, who, as if possessed
Of Satan, labors with success
To fool the public through the press,
And broadcast through the country strews
Installments large of bogus news.

Thank Providence we don't belong
To those who thusly have gone wrong.
The fakir's dodges ne'er come nigh
Our haunts—We cannot tell a lie.
Full often with our little ax
We lay folks prostrate in their tracks;
And if we're charged with talking bosh,
We use the words of young G. Wash.
So, mark you, in a special way .
We seek to celebrate the day
Devoted to that noble youth
Who slung an ax and told the truth.

ELECTION NIGHT.

At last we've reached election eve,
    And some are glad,
    And some are sad.
Hearts throb apace for Cleve and Steve,
    Or palpitate for Ben.
The wisest can't exactly guess
    What fate's decree
    Is booked to be.
And hope is mingled with distress
    'Mid stalwart party men.

B. H. is strong; why should we fear
    That in the fray
    Collapse he may,
Since aptly he knows how to steer
    The gallant ship of state?
But, bless you, there are turns and tricks
    In ev'ry trade
    Adroitly made,
And thus, in this confounded mix,
    He may capitulate.

Per contra, there's no reason why
      G. C. should dupe
      Us all and scoop
The pot, although the public eye
      Sees where.his hand is weak.
Yet Grove has sharpers at his back,
      Who know enough
      With skill to bluff,
And threaten now the cards to "stack"—
      How's that for icy cheek?

Election bets amount to "nix."
      The "gams," you'll find
      Must go it blind.
And while one-half get in their licks
      The other half get left.
And he who blows his horn the most
      Will, like as not,
      Be nicely caught,
And feel like giving up the ghost
      When of his pile bereft.

Alas! that in this age of guile
      And irksome doubt
      We are without
An oracle of Delphic style
      To give us tips exact!
But failing this, what can we do
      Except to wait
      And speculate?
So, till the voters all get through,
      We'll do the anxious act.

51

COLUMBUS.

Bring the good old Caravel across the
    seas, yeo-ho!
Bring her as she first was brought four
    hundred years ago,
When she came for Yankeeland a-hunting
    high and low,
    Thanks to the nerve of Columbus.

Chorus.

Hurrah, hurrah! Let's sing the praise of
    Chris.
Hurrah, hurrah! Just think what we
    would miss
If Chris had never stumbled on a land so
    fair as this;
    That's what we owe to Columbus.

In the town of Genoa Columbus first drew
    breath.
People there still ask you, "Didgenoabout
    his death?"
For he is forgotten there; so many an ex-
    pert saith;
    That's pretty rough on Columbus.

Pedagogues insisted that the earth was
    wholly flat;
Christopher declared he couldn't let it
    go at that.
Thereupon the nincompoops with big rat-
    tans got at
And tanned the hide of Columbus.

Christopher grew up and went a-sailing
    on the sea.
"In the course of time I'll knock out Cap-
    tain Cook," thought he.
Cook had not been born yet, but the gift
    of prophecy
Lurked in the soul of Columbus.

Isabella met the lad (she was the Queen
    of Spain);
Thought he was dead gone on her, for
    Belle was pretty vain.
"Christopher," she said, "for thee my bank
    account I'll drain."
Right in the swim was Columbus.

Bella she put up the cash; Columbus did
    the rest;
Sailed away from Palos toward the undis-
    covered west.
Everybody thought the scheme was but
    a merry jest;
But they were fooled in Columbus.

Glorious the triumph was when Yankee-
    land he struck,
Filled with copper-colored folks and lots
    of garden truck.
"Gentlemen," says Christopher, "this is a
    run of luck."
Those were the words of Columbus.

Other foreign immigrants came after,
    when they saw
That the Indians didn't have a contract la-
    bor law;
Hence the Union flourishes with more or
    less eclat,
All on account of Columbus.

Therefore join us, young and old, and
    make the welkin ring.
Hymns of jubilation let us all in chorus
    sings.
Thankful for the good things that continue
    still to spring
Out of the cruise of Columbus.

THE SOUTHERN CAVALIER.

Come hither, ye people, and hear us sing
The tale of ye knighte Sir Henry King.

A doughty cavalier was he,
And he lived in the state of Tennessee.

Sir Henry's middle name was Clay,
And he moistened the same the livelong
    day.

For in Tennessee there is no lack
Of the good old Bourbon tamarack.

And when Sir Henry a jaglet wore,
He was ready for barrels of human gore.

Spear and buckler he did not don,
For those things out of fashion had gone.

But to cope with bluster and idle vaunts,
He carried a gun in his knightly pants.

And hostilities came to a sudden stop
Whenever Sir Henry got the drop.

Posten he was an esquire plain,
Who practiced law for the sake of gain.

He plead the case of a wounded dove,
Who had been Sir Henry's light o' love.

For her the knight, of his senses stripped,
Away from his wife and babes had
    skipped.

And now her return for his conduct rash
Was to capture the whole of his ready
    cash.

Posten rebuked the knight in style,
And proved that he was a scoundrel vile.

"I' faith," said the knight, with his teeth
    tight set,
"I'll have revenge upon Posten yet."

So he waited without in the public street,
And laid the esquire dead at his feet.

Yeomen came in coats of blue
And led off the knight without much ado.

The courts they hastened the case to try,
And informed Sir Henry that he must die.

And so this knight of the race of King
Was doomed on the gallows tree to swing.

Unexpectedly into the game
The governor, Baron Buchanan, came.

Says he, "By my halidome, this won't do,
The blood of the Kings is of azure hue.

"And why should Sir Henry be undone
For the chivalrous use of his little gun?

"Is southern chivalry dead that thus
The gallows must gobble the cream of us?

"No, no; to hang an aristocrat
Is a positive crime; I'll have none of that."

That settled the case; Sir Henry then
Went off pro tem. to a cell in the "pen."

From which in the course of time, no
    doubt,
His friends will see that he's pardoned
    out.

Nobility thus a victory won,
While the band played "Johnny, Get Your
    Gun."

And southern cavaliers wept for joy
To think they could still their foes de-
    stroy.

Howls went up from a violent mob,
Which claimed the thing was a lawless
    job.

But folks who haven't a family tree
Amount to nothing in Tennessee.

Hence Baron Buchanan and his compeers,
Rejoicing, tackled the cup that cheers.

And they put a sign on the gallows high:
"No blooded murderers need apply."

MISCELLANEOUS.

CHAUTAUQUA.

Chautauqua! O thou sacred spot,
Where idle tourists linger not;
Where vulgar sports, of habits low,
Their brazen faces never show;
Where fakirs for their arts profane
A license ask, but ask in vain;
And where enlightened laws exclude
The noxious lady-killing dude;
The vivid fact we can't disguise—
Thou art a Christian paradise.

Pure are the ways thou walkest in,
Unlike those garish haunts of sin,
Seaside resorts, where throng like sheep
The vulgar, making angels weep.
Tom, Dick and Harry there combine
To soak themselves with rosy wine.
Along the beach the maidens scoot,
Each in a scanty bathing suit.
The righteous man, with burning cheek,
Must turn from these thy charms to seek.

Lo, in thy temples do we find
Sublime reflection for the mind.
Thy people nearly all possess
A score of titles, more or less.
Doctors, Professors, Reverends, too,
In all directions are on view;
And every one his chance doth wait
To mount the platform and orate.
Thine is, in fact, Chautauqua dear,
A most didactic atmosphere.

Rostrums and blackboards huge abound;
They're utilized by thinkers sound;
Philosophers with heads that bulge,
Who scientific truths divulge;
Linguists well versed in ev'ry freak
Of Latin, Hebrew, French and Greek;
Artistic sharps who'd have you know
That they could teach Mike Angelo.
Glory is theirs that never fades
In blest Chautauqua's classic shades.

The woman on the suffrage lay—
Of course, you know, "she'd-talk-away,"
And so she does. Her light's not hid,
For John stays home to mind the kid,
And while his hand the cradle rocks
She lectures on the ballot box.
This feat, so woman-like and cute,
Brings forth the handkerchief salute,
And as the girls the speaker greet,
They vow Chautauqua's "just too sweet."

Alas, Chautauqua, with distress
The ghastly truth we must confess,
With thee and thine we can't consort,
Because on goodness we are short.
Excuse our conscienceless remarks,
But we prefer midsummer larks
To hearing the discourse complex
Of Doctor Y. or Reverend X.
Therefore, thy charms with reverend awe
We'll worship from afar.
                                        Ta, ta.

THE BARBER.

Victim in the barber shop
Has a heavy thatch on top;
Has a crop of whisker rough,
Wants to have 'em both cut off.
Peels off collar, coat and vest,
Lets the barber do the rest.

Barber takes his prey in tow,
Oils his tongue and lets her go,
Hopes the razor doesn't pull,
Tells of happ'nings wonderful;
Baseball records, foreign wars,
Habits of the planet Mars.

Tariff schedules new and old
He is happy to unfold;
(Seafoam, sir? What, no? Then do
Try my extra-fine shampoo'');
Freaks of great men he'll recite
With unlimited delight.

Boxing? He is quite at home
In the latest hippodrome.
Yachts? What need to say that he
Knows their points like A, B, C.
(Cut her close, sir? Ah, just so),
Bless us, how his tongue does go!

Messages from Cleveland's pen,
Scandals in the Upper Ten,
Newest dramas on the stage,
Songs that have become the rage;
(Part it on the side, you say?")
Thus the barber pounds away.

Victim stands it all he can,
Bears up like a little man;
Barber's talk he can't avoid,
Doesn't want to be destroyed;
("Now, sir; wax on your mustache?")
Victim's done and pays his cash.

Barber, barber, some fine day
Justice will assert her sway;
Then to keep you clear of crime
You'll be muzzled all the time.
Think of this next time and spare
Captives in your fatal chair.

61

TWO LITTLE GIRLS BLEW IN.

An old man's nephew conversed one day
  With his uncle, a stager old,
Who had formerly been on the am'rous
    lay,
  But whose ardor had now grown cold.
"My boy," quoth the unc., "hear the
    mournful tale
Of two of your kith and kin,
Whose marital hopes were of no avail
  Till two little girls blew in.

Refrain.

Two little girls blew in, lad,
  Two little girls blew in.
We were brothers, they were sisters,
  Each of 'em was a twin.
Two little girls blew in, lad,
  And here's where there came a hitch,
    None could without bother
    Tell one from the other,
  And few could tell whom was which.

We all fell in love in a mutual style,
  Pledges we interchanged.
Fortune upon us was fain to smile,
  And the weddings were soon arranged.
But, lad, in the hurry and bustle and whirl
  At the church—'twas a shame and a
    sin—
Each one of us married the other one's
    girl,
  When two little girls blew in.

    Ref.—Two little girls blew in, etc.

What could we do in this terrible plight?
  Ah, lad, 'twas a trial sore.
We went to Chicago that very same night
  And got a divorce for four.
'Twas mournful to think of the time we
    had lost
  In our efforts those brides to win,
Little knowing how sadly our lives would
    be crossed
  When two little girls blew in.

    Ref.—Two little girls blew in, etc.

But stay—there's a sequel—whene'er we
    got back,
  And the torrents of tears had dried,
We somehow resumed the original track,
  And for marital bliss we sighed.
So we shuffled the pair, and quick as a
    flash
  Each wedded a blooming twin.
And 'twas awful the total of honeymoon
    cash
  Those two little girls blew in."

    Ref.—Two little girls blew in, etc.

    —*With apologies to " Two Little Girls in Blue '*

63

ST. VALENTINE.

St. Valentine, St. Valentine,
In former days you used to shine
　　With glory that was splendid;
But in these sordid modern days
No longer does your glory blaze,
　　Your day is nearly ended.

No more the maid who's badly mashed
Waits eagerly and unabashed
　　Your long-expected coming.
And when the postman heaves in sight
Jumps up to meet him with delight
　　And heart insanely drumming.

No more she looks for Cupid's darts,
Transfixing lovers' bleeding hearts
　　With verses printed under;
Nor views the lace and satin fair,
The silver, gold and colors rare
　　With ecstasy and wonder.

No Strephon who for her doth pine
Sends in an elegant design
    Of unexampled value,
Conveying in its ins and outs
The sighs of "Streph," the fears, the
        doubts,
    The "will you?" and the "shall you?"

No, no, at most she gets a screed
That makes her furious, indeed,
    A "comic" most insulting,
That treads upon her tender toes,
And indicates that ugly foes
    Are o'er her faults exulting.

Perhaps it shows a wall-flower lone,
A scrawny frame of skin and bone
    And corkscrew curls to match it,
And says "This hatchet-faced old thing
Will never wear a wedding ring;
    No man would care to catch it."

Or else mayhap in manner gross
It loads her down with adipose
    And pictures standing round her
A gaping crowd of jays that cry
"Get on to this. Who'll buy; who'll buy
    The sixteen hundred pounder?"

And Strephon by some rascal rude
Will be depicted as a dude,
    All clothes with nothing in 'em;
A dawd er on the avenue
Who looks for lovely girls to woo
    His precious self and win him.

Such is the dire and painful pass
To which the valentine, alas,
    Has come. Oh, 'tis a pity
That love no more the artist's hand
Directs and turns out verses grand,
    Harmonious, chaste and witty.

St. Valentine, St. Valentine,
Your pearls are cast these days to swine,
    Go seek your final slumber;
For wherefore strive and strive and strive
To keep your vital spark alive
    When you're an old back number?

THE HOLIDAYS.

The holidays, the holidays!
O days of love and joy and praise,
When every heart with warmth expands
And time hangs lightly on our hands;
When people young and old unite
In wild, hilarious delight;
When enemies lay down the sword
And heave their quarrels overboard;
There's music in the very phrase—
"The holidays, the holidays!"

The holidays, the holidays!
'Tis then that in a thousand ways
The merchant stimulates surprise
If he knows how to advertise.
A sled, a drum, a pair of skates
With ev'ry purchase he donates;
Sells books for nothing (generous cuss!)
And grows almost delirious.
He'll tell you, if you ask what pays—
"The holidays, the holidays!"

The holidays, the holidays!
Who is too poor to make a raise
And blow it in, with secret glee,
On trimmings for the Christmas tree;
On gifts to gratify the whim
Of Kittie, Mollie, Tom and Jim.
Slippers for dad, a chain for ma,
And something cheap for mother-in-law?
What causes all this giving craze?
The holidays, the holidays!

The holidays, the holidays!
With happiness they fairly blaze.
See Santa Claus, with skip and hop,
Cavorting tow'rds the chimney top,
While little folks in cosy beds
Beneath the comforts hide their heads,
And older ones with dread are racked
While doing the Chriskingle act.
List to the rattle of the sleighs!—
The holidays, the holidays!

The holidays, the holidays!
The mem'ry of them with us stays;
A gilt-edged mem'ry, strangely dear
(We've got to wax pathetic here;
For pathos is a simple ruse
That Christmas poets always use)—
Aye, faith, Horatio, many a one
Will miss these pleasures when he's gone.
Lead on, then, to the giddy maze—
The holidays, the holidays!

67

IRENE'S VOW.

Irene MacWelsh was passing fair,
  All hearts she took by storm;
Her moral character was square
  And rounded was her form.

Two lovers her young heart addressed;
  Two handsome, winsome "beauts";
Their Sunday suits they first got pressed,
  And then they pressed their suits.

One was De Smith, a youth who throve
  As teller in a bank.
Says he, "I'll tell 'er of my love
  And win 'er with my rank."

The other was De Jones, a spry
  Young lawyer erudite.
Quoth he, "I'll win the case if I
  Acquit myself aright."

Now Irene took to sobs and sighs,
  To choose, the girl was loth,
For—not to deal in idle lies—
  She idolized them both.

De Smith waxed hot; De Jones grew
    wrath,
  In unison they cried:
"Two hands to give the lady hath,
  But how her heart divide?"

Then did those youths find out a way
  Their troubles to dispel;
A duel would, so reasoned they,
  Duelegantly well.

Unto the football field they bent
  Their steps and bent 'em straight
To where a very large per cent.
  Of heroes met their fate.

Their weapons were' the flying wedge,
  The tackle and the punt,
Of footfalls heavy as a sledge
  Each bore the murd'rous brunt.

Soon, soon the bloody fray was o'er,
  The ball had crossed the goal,
And both the youths lay in their gore,
  With not a bone left whole.

Friends told Irene about the fray,
  How, in the wild attack,
The twain who had been whole one day
  The next came not half-back.

Stunned by the blow, the maiden said:
  "'Tis I that slew those men;
Henceforth on thorns will be my bed,
  I'll ne'er touch down again."

69

LULLABY.

Over the mountains to Booze-Away Land,
    Bye-bye, bye-bye,
Where fairies are sporting on Tamarack
    strand,
    Bye-bye, bye-bye.
Weary eyes closing and legs getting weak
Tongue getting thick—ah, 'tis hard now to
    speak,
Papa's been on it, dear babe, for a week
    Bye-bye, bye-bye.

Daily he trudges to Barrelhouse Town,
    Bye-bye, bye-bye.
His nose it is red and his taste is sea
    brown,
    Bye-bye, bye-bye.
Bright is the sheen of the dollars he
    spends,
Setting 'em up for his thousands of
    friends;
A white-aproned goblin upon him attends
    Bye-bye, bye-bye.

Alcohol River's aglow in the sun,
    Bye-bye, bye-bye.
Dad goes a-swimmin' when he has the
  "mon,"
    Bye-bye, bye-bye.
Rivulets enter its bosom so clear,
Rhine wine, and claret, ale, porter and
  beer,
But King Corn-Juice lays over 'em all,
  never fear,
    Bye-bye, bye-bye.

See where the boas and copperheads play,
    Bye-bye, bye-bye;
Always frisk round when the old man's
  that way,
    Bye-bye, bye-bye.
Take him away where the Strait Jack-
  ets dwell,
Into a cute little Hospital Cell;
Medical fairies will soon make him well,
    Bye-bye, bye-bye.

Grand is the Kingdom of Do-It-No-More,
    Bye-bye, bye-bye,
Dad will land there when the circus is
  o'er,
    Bye-bye, bye-bye.
O little babe, when to manhood you grow,
Never to Booze-Away Land must you go;
Look at your father, and tell me "No, no!"
    Bye-bye, bye-bye.

THE KEELEYITES.

Yesterday with faces shining,
Never the slightest bit repining
For the days when they were wining
  And rampaging round at nights.
In the baking, broiling weather,
Out to Oakland all together,
In the very highest feather
  Came the noble Keeleyites.

Some could not refrain from thinking
Of the fun they had in drinking,
At saloonists slyly winking,
  (Those were genuine delights.)
Lager beer and Roman punches,
Juleps, slings and barroom lunches,
Soon would render quite unconscious
  Those who now are Keeleyites.

Medford rum and brandy smashes
Absinthe gulped in modest dashes,
(Don't you think a fellow rash is
    Who his brain with these excites?)
Cocktails, cobblers, Tom and Jerry,
Claret, port, champagne and sherry,
All were guzzled by the merry
    Chaps who now are Keeleyites.

Thus they'd go ahead competing,
Everyone the other treating
Till they'd have no time for eating,
    Nor for aught but crazy flights.
Every night would find them staving,
Ripping, roaring, ranting, raving
And outrageously behaving,
    Those who now are Keeleyites.

Finally their blood relations
Tired of furious demonstrations,
Would suspend recriminations
    And let up on useless fights.
To the hospital they'd hurry,
Make the topers thither scurry,
Hoping thus to end their worry
    With the future Keeleyites.

All this nonsense now is ended,
Since the "topes" their way have
    wended
To the place where Keeley's splendid
    Method gets 'em dead to rights.
No more wine for them or liquors,
They are stayers, aye and stickers,
Regular sober old jimslickers
    Are those noble Keeleyites.

IN OLE KAINTUCK.

Dar's ole Bill Breckinridge a-settin' up in
    co't
  Wid people all admirin' him bekase he
    am so smart;
His ha'r am white, but old Billy am a
    spo't;
  Mos' ebry pretty gal he sees plays hob
    wid Billy's heart.
If de gal escapes, she's got a heap o' luck,
Dat's de way we does down in old Kain-
    tuck.

Dar's young Mattie Pollard, jes' as sweet
    as any peach,
  She caught old Mistah Bill mighty easy
    on de fly,
W'en he sez "I love yo'" Mattie didn't
    screech,
  She jes' sez "Willyum, no odah need
    apply."
Each on de odah one immegiuntly wuz
    struck,
Dat's de way we does down in old Kain-
    tuck.

W'en ole Bill wuz widdered, Mattie
    bought a little gun,
"Willyum," sez she, "Don't yo' tink we
    oughter wed?"
Sez ole Bill to Mat, "Well dis kind er
    takes de bun;
    Marry you I won't, gal, so don' yo' lose
      yo' head."
At dat Mattie's gun undah ole Bill's nose
    she stuck,
Dat's de way we does down in old Kain-
    tuck.

Ole Bill wuz scart; his face turned w'ite
    as snow,
"Mattie," sez he, "I'm not ready yet ter
    die,
If I mus' be yo' husband an' no longer be
    yo' beau,
    Drop dat 'ar gun, an' de weddin' ring
      I'll buy."
De ole man, yo' see, 'gainst a weppin
    couldn't buck,
Dat's de way we does down in old Kain-
    tuck.

Nex' t'ing yo' know, ole Bill he skips
    away;
    Gibs de gal de shake an' gets himself a
    wife,
"Well an' good," says Mat, "Now I t'ink
    de propah lay
    Is ter reach fo' Willyum's cash, 'stead
      ob Willyum's useless life;"
So Mattie hired a lawyah her Willyum's
    wings ter pluck,
Dat's de way we does down in ole Kain-
    tuck.

Now dey's in de co't-rcom, both a bilin'
    mad,
    Mat she tells on Bill and Bill he tells
    on Mat,
Oh, dem co't-room stories am real, real
    bad,
    ut all dem long-faced Christyuns seem
    awful glad ob dat.
Maybe dey de case out de winder soon
    will chuck,
Dat's de way we does down in ole Kain-
    tuck.

PADDYWHISKY.

A strain of mourning fills the air; a strain
    of anguish keen,
Because the god-like maestro has vanished
    from the scene.
Unto their grief our Pittsburg maids un-
    ceasingly give vent,
The world for them has lost its charm
    since
                 Paddy
                     Whisky
                          Went.

The mem'ry of his tawny hair is like a
    bushy dream.
Three feet of wiry waviness—a poet's fit-
    ting theme.
Out, out upon close-shaven heads! Who
    cares a copper cent
For ordinary barber work since
                 Paddy
                     Whisky
                          Went?

His features they are classic, and he has
  a melting eye;
He doesn't wear a spiketail coat like any
  common guy;
His limblets are a poem, in their move-
  ments eloquent,
We'll never see their like again since
                Paddy
                  Whisky
                        Went.

They say he plays sonatas and symphonic
  thingumbobs,
Which move expert musicians to indulge
  in pray'rs and sobs;
But music doesn't enter to a very great
  extent
Into what the girls are thinking of since
                Paddy
                  Whisky
                        Went.

O ye who at his altar have been
  worshiping, suppose
The whole ecstatic crowd go after "Pad"
  where'er he goes.
'Tis only thus that kindred souls forever
  can be blent
And wipe out all the pangs one feels since
                Paddy
                  Whisky
                        Went.

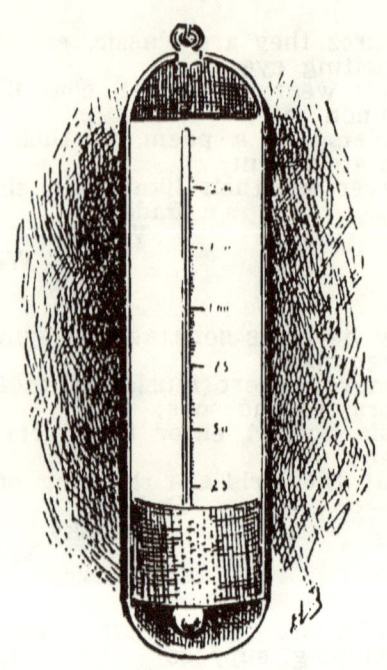

BALLADE.

'Tis the fashion in the theaters in plain-
    tive tones to sing
  Of antiquities that reverence compel.
There's the "hat me father wore" and
    grandma's matrimonial ring,
  And the oaken bucket hanging in the
    well.
There is grandpa's eight-day clock and
    some one else's baby shoe;
  Shaky tenors love these relics to recall;
But we've got a little token that can all
    of them outdo—
  Our thermometer that hangs upon the
    wall.

Refrain.

Touch it gently; handle it with care;
  Spurn it not, whatever may befall.
Though 'tis knock-kneed now and crazy,
Yet it used to be a daisy—
  Our thermometer that hangs upon the
    wall.

Ah! how well do we remember when a
quarter we blew in
For that instrument—'twas many years
ago.
Mother met us with a gurgle, and said father with a grin,
"Bless you, lad, the heat henceforth
we'll always know."
On the porch we hung it proudly—there
a splendid show it made,
And the spectacle the neighbors did en-
thral,
For it registered immediately two hundred
in the shade—
Our thermometer that hangs upon the
wall.

Ref.—Touch it gently, etc.

When the cruel winter came and brought
along the snow and ice,
Ninety-nine below the zero mark it
showed.
You can bet we wouldn't sell it then—no,
not for any price,
For with pride our system fairly over-
flowed.
Weather experts tried to down us, and
gave lying figures out;
Their audacity was such as to appall;
But our friends would not go back on us
—not one of 'em would doubt
Our thermometer that hangs upon the
wall.

Ref.—Touch it gently, etc.

In the end there came a scorcher; 'twas
a broiling August day,
And the mercury the "boiling point" had
passed;
But it couldn't stand the pressure, and to
every one's dismay
The thermometer was busted up at last.
Bitter, bitter were our tears as with the
keenest of regret
Old Infallible we hastened to install
In a place of lasting honor—and 'tis there
you'll see it yet—
Our thermometer that hangs upon the
wall.

Ref.—Touch it gently, etc.

SMILING SPRING.

'Tis bound to come; we can't refrain
　From grinding out a merry strain
　　About the smiling spring.
For, after many a chill rebuff,
We've weather now that's not a bluff,
But bona fide vernal stuff,
　　The regulation thing.

No more at morn a polar breeze
Makes finger-tips and noses freeze
　　And vegetation nips.
No more good wives are lost in doubt,
If they shall get their fire screens out
Or put the dust and dirt to rout,
　　And husbands thus eclipse.

Behold, the festive bock beer sign
　Gets thirsty topers right in line—
　　The prancing goat they hail.
Saloonists hang out doors of green,
The druggist works his fizz machine
And hankey-pankey men are seen
　　With mystic stuff for sale.

Light-coated dudes together flock;
(Their winter clothing is in hock),
    Their looks a smile invite.
In tailors' windows cards appear,
"Three-dollar pantaloonings here,"
Or "Coatings less than cost"—'tis clear
    They're strictly out of sight.

Policemen on their corners doze
And dream of donning lighter clothes,
    With helmets made to match.
The letter carrier hums a tune;
He'll wear a fragile duster soon,
For which as a superior boon
    He's now upon the watch.

Suburban residents go wild,
By seedsmen's gorgeous ads beguiled,
    And dig and rake like mad.
Unhappy folk, how sad 'twill be
When of their work the fruits they see,
Which somehow will not seem to gee
    With any seedsman's ad!

The farmer—pessimistic chap—
Arises from his winter nap,
    And navigates the plow;
Puts in preliminary crops,
Works day and night and never stops
Unless a moment while he mops
    His overheated brow.

The trees put on their choicest duds,
By which we mean the leaves and buds:
    Small flow'rs stick up their heads
The birds, with furtive looks of gloom,
Get up a secret building boom,
Domestic cares they will assume,
    When each the other weds.

And human lovers—here we stick;
The subject always makes us sick;
    No Tennyson in ours.
The signs we've given should suffice
To prove that spring's no more on ice,
But serves to-day an extra slice
    Of sunshine and of flow'rs.

81

JUNE.

Bright month of June, to thee we sing,
  Two days ahead of time,
Because our artist's taken wing,
And left us not a blessed thing
  On which to build a rhyme,
  Except a likeness fair to see
  Of thee, sweet June, of thee.

O sunny June, we love to view
  The roses on thy cheek;
And feel thy genial warmth anew,
For May has made us mighty blue—
  Each day it sprang a leak.
  So if with joy you'd fill our cup,
  Dry up, sweet June, dry up.

O lively June—convention days
 'Tis thine to bring along;
What time the politicians raise
Partic'lar Cain, and Matthew Quay's
 Mailed hand controls the throng.
 This year you must keep clear of Matt,
 Mark that, sweet June, mark that.

O festive June—when, dropping book
 And slate, Young Hopeful hails
Vacation—need he now play hook?
Not so, to thee he'll gladly look
 As one whose aid avails
 To bring eight weeks of solid fun.
 Well done, sweet June, well done.

O kindly June—please don't forget
 To bring us summer heat.
Straw hats are 'neath a cloud as yet,
And no one has a chance to sweat;
 In fact by Prob we're beat.
 So, inasmuch as that's a sin,
 Pile in, sweet June, pile in.

83

PICNIC SEASON.

Now the picnic season's starting
  And on ev'ry side you'll see
People merrily departing,
  Bound to sport upon the lea.
What the lea may be we dare not
  Give away to any one.
More than this to say we care not:
  'Tis the thing they'll sport upon.

Lads and lasses, free from sadness,
  Will together dance and sing;
Yes, with ditties full of gladness
  They will make the welkin ring.
Of the welkin do not ask us
  If the meaning we'll expound,
Cruelly the same would task us,
  For to secrecy we're bound.

Mr. Strephon (sly persuader)
Will with Phyllis press his suit,
And perhaps he'll serenade her
Very neatly on his lute.
Of the lute to˜get a notion
The desire you may indulge,
But we answer with emotion
That we really can't divulge.

Lemonade will flow profusely,
And so dry will be a few
That they'll liquor up quite loosely,
As the dryads used to do.
Maybe some one will be asking
What's a dryad, anyhow?
But our duty the unmasking
Of this myst'ry won't allow.

Yes, those picnics are delightful
In a multitude of ways;
Do away with feelings spiteful,
And make happy halcyon days.
As to halcyon—pray be lenient,
Ask us not to make it clear,
For we're making it convenient
To wind up the lyric here.

AUTUMN.

What ho, there, varlet! hither bring
  The quinine flask inviting,
For in my bones I feel the sting
  Of blasts both cold and biting.
Old Sol, you see, has slid away
  (He's somehow slipped his tether),
And in his stead there's come to stay
  Bleak, damp, autumnal weather.

My pills? Ah, yes, these are the stuff
  To knock out chills and fever.
My doctor gives 'em many a puff,
  And Doc. is no deceiver.
Here's the prescription, writ with skill
  (Ah, Doc., I am your debtor):
"Two pillulae each hour until
  The patient's feeling better."

My plasters? Yes, just stick them on
  My shoulders, sides and middle—
They toast a fellow, every one,
  Like cakes upon the griddle.
A royal thing a plaster is
  To aid the renovation
Of one who has the rheumatiz
  And needs some lubrication.

Hot water? Certainly, my lad,
  And put some mustard in it.
The foot-bath treatment isn't bad,
  And wherefore not begin it?
I'd rather be fried, steamed and boiled,
  Stewed, roasted, swathed and sweated,
Greased, buttered, tarred and carbon-oiled,
  Than die and be regretted.

But stay—the punch? Oh, happy thought,
  Where is my friendly flagon?
Don't tell me that one never ought
  To get a quiet jag on.
Hot punch? What else in all this land
  Can beat it? Oh, my brothers,
As long as we've this cure on hand,
  Away with all the others.

THE WAGNER ERA.

Our town is progressing, they tell us,
  In thoroughbred musical taste,
And people are getting more zealous
  In studying harmonies chaste.
Dutch street bands are wholly demolished,
  Cheap harpists have fled far away,
And the hand-organ fiend is abolished,
  For culture is coming to stay.

The minstrel show's left us forever
  ('Tis utterly vulgar, you know).
The ditties we used to think clever
  Are scouted as trashy and low.
The melodies of the plantation,
  Which made quite a hit in their day,
Now are said to involve degradation,
  For culture is coming to stay.

No more do we hear "Suwanee River,"
  And the "Sweet Bye and Bye" has gone
    hence;
"Annie Laurie" makes classicists shiver—
  To sing it's a penal offense.
"Home, Sweet Home," there's no use in
    performing;
  The warbler thereof is a jay;
He would simply set critics a-storming,
  For culture is coming to stay.

If your end you would socially keep up,
  And move in an elegant sphere,
Your heart must delightedly leap up
  When Wagner's productions you hear.
"Goetterdaemmerung" must be your Bible,
  "Walkyrie" your passions must sway;
Simple tunes are on music a libel,
  For culture is coming to stay.

Comic opera always a scandal
  And curse to the world you must vote;
Just tolerate Mozart and Handel
  And the little things Beethoven wrote.
Bear in mind that a strict sense of duty
  Compels you contempt to display
For J. L. Molloy and Pinsuti,
  Since culture is coming to stay.

Now 'tis true that the goal is still distant,
  Some hanker for melody yet,
But by patience and labor persistent,
  At length to a point we will get,
Where in technique and art contrapuntal
  We'll all be professionals gay,
And the critics no more we'll disgruntle,
  For culture is coming to stay.

89

THE BOY GRADUATE.

He mounts the stage. His brow is clear,
He knows no qualm, no puny fear,
    No quiver of dismay.
Noble and lofty is the state
Of youthful Mr. Graduate
    Upon commencement day.

Garments brand-new his form bedeck,
A tow'ring collar walls his neck,
    His cuffs are snowy white.
Who, in such radiant togs as these,
Could stoop to weak'ning at the knees,
    Beset with vulgar fright?

Not he. The proud and happy lad
Expertly coached and nobly clad,
    Feels "to the manor born."
Genius his soaring soul expands,
And fame nearby awaiting stands—
    He views the mob with scorn.

What's this that he unfolds? Oh, ye
It is, it is, a large MS.,
    With burning thoughts inscribed.
The people listen with intense
Delight, till all his eloquence
    They've joyously imbibed.

All nature's secrets he unlocks,
The rules of science orthodox
    He handles like a sage.
Problems that make our statesmen swear
He settles with astuteness rare
    In this benighted age.

Then, when the thunders of applause
Have ceased, and he at length withdraws,
    'Mid torrents of bouquets,
The glee club claims him, and he takes
His turn at rippling trills and shakes
    In rattling college lays.

Alas! that after college days,
With light and life and hope ablaze,
    There comes a cold, cold deal;
When heroes of the stage must try
Their luck at hustling, or—oh, my!—
    Go join a "Commonweal."

THE GIRL GRADUATE.

What form is this whose charms serene,
With delicate and lustrous sheen,
   The stage illuminate?
Is't Venus or Diana? Nay,
'Tis one far lovelier than they—
   The sweet girl graduate.

In robes of virgin white she stands,
With jewels on her dainty hands,
   And flow'rets in her hair.
Her glass has told her of her charms,
And so she feels no strange alarms,
   Nor shirks the footlights' glare.

A thousand dudes in yellow shoes,
And neckties of hilarious hues,
   Look on with lovesick eyes.
Their gaze she does not fear to meet,
But just to bring them to her feet
   Her level b.. :... tries.

A hush upon the audience falls,
Deep interest its soul enthralls,
    No covert sneer doth lurk
When she unties a ribbon blue,
And opens up to public view
    Her essay—peerless work!

Now, now she lets the torrents loose
Of learning vast, and thoughts abstruse,
    Worthy of sages old.
The field of rhetoric for flow'rs
She ransacks. Wondrous are the pow'rs
    That here themselves unfold.

Scarce have the plaudits died away,
When lo! she seats herself to play
    Piano solos grand;
Mozart, Tschaikowsky, Sydney Smith,
She bangs and slams and rattles with
    A finely cultured hand.

She closes. Flow'rs fall round her fast,
How can she ever be outclassed?
    Folks ask with flushing cheek.
Ask of young Counter Jumper who
Gets twelve per month, his honest due:
    She'll marry him next week.

ODE TO AN UMBRELLA.

Hail, old umbrella! Tempest-scarred
  And wobbly as thou art,
One cannot help but view thee, pard,
  With kindliness of heart.

Although thy ribs are out of gear,
  Although thy coat is torn,
For thee there is no covert sneer,
  No epithet of scorn.

For, in thy old age, thou art proof
  Against the itching hands
That somehow can ne'er hold aloof
  From one's umbrella-stands.

In railway trains thou mayst be left,
  Untouched by those that loot.
Thy owner cannot be bereft
  Of thee, old parachute.

If thou wert made of silken stuff,
  With silver mountings gay,
Thieves could not hurry fast enough
  To carry thee away.

But, old "umbrell," the duty's thine
  To hold thy place as yet,
To travel with us when 'tis fine
  And vanish when 'tis wet.

At home in leisure thou shalt lie,
  When rain begins to pour,
But when there is a cloudless sky,
  Be always to the fore.

Such is thy custom, aged gamp—
  With innocence demure,
To hide thyself in weather damp,
  And hold a sinecure.

But, bless thy ancient heart, why not
  Thus slumber on the shelf?
If we were an "umbrell," that's what
  We'd like to do ourself.

THE MANDOLIN CLUB.

O list to the music that's borne on a
 breeze,
 (Tink-a-tink, tink-a-tunk, tink-a-tay);
Like the ripple of wavelets on sweet sum-
 mer seas
 (Tink-a-tonk, tink-a-tank, tink-a-too);
No semblance of discord the harmony
 warps,
One would think 'twas the angels per-
 forming on harps,
But 'tis only a concert of mandolin sharps
 (Twink-a-twank, twink-a-twunk, twink-
 a-twee).

Refrain.

Then hearken with rapture beyond all
 compare,
To the sweet twinkle-twankling that
 twunks through the air.
Flee away from the brass band's delirious
 blare,
 And the orchestra's giddy hubbub.

Dull care to the winds will at once be
consigned,
And a solace for grief you'll immediately
find,
In the gentle and soft twinkle-twankle-
some grind
Of the twunklesome Mandolin club.
(Twink-a-twoo.)

Beethoven's sonatas they play like old
vets
And full justice they do to the "High
School Cadets"
(Tink-a-tonk, tink-a-tank, tink-a-too);
The waltzes of Strauss and Waldteufel
they play
In a witchingly winsome and delicate
way;
Till you wish they'd keep at it all night
and all day.
(Twink-a-twank, twink-a-twunk, twink-
a-twee).

Ref.—Then hearken with rapture, etc.

The "Dead March in Saul" they can ren-
der with skill
(Tink-a-tink, tink-a-tunk, tink-a-tay);
And the strains of the "Yorke" they reel
off with a will
(Tink-a-tonk, tink-a-tank, tink-a-too);
"McGinty," "Tannhauser," the songs of
the war,
"Semiramide," "White Wings" and "Rory
O'More,"
Are among the bright things in their vast
repertoire.
(Twink-a-twank, twink-a-twunk, twink-
a-twee).

Ref.—Then hearken with rapture, etc.

Pianos and organs must move to the rear
(Tink-a-tink, tink-a-tunk, tink-a-tay);
Their light is bedimmed while the mando-
lin's here
(Tink-a- nk, tink-a-tank, tink-a-too);
The future May Festival, all must agree,
Will be shaped to conform to the people's
decree,
And a mandolin carnival surely 'twill be
(Twink-a-twank, twink-a-twunk, twink-
a-twee).

Ref.—Then hearken with rapture, etc.

THE PUNSTER.

There was a jolly Irish lad,
  Who hailed from down in Munster.
He met with influences bad,
  And thus became a punster.
Like poor Tom Hood, whene'er he spoke,
  Facetiously he would wink,
And with some light and playful joke
  The populace he'd Hood-wink.

The doings of the dentist's ax
  To him were ax-i-dental,
The feeling toward a landlord's tax
  He looked on as pa(y)rental.
The undertaker he'd remind
  That death would overtake him;
The final sleep one's eyes might blind,
  And yet this man would "wake" him.

Napoleon Bonaparte, he said,
  Was just a Water-loser;
A jimjam victim's bugaboos
  Just marked the bugaboozer.
Ben Butler's eye, he said, was like
  A pistol, since he cocked it.
With stones a babe he would not strike,
  Although he sometimes "rocked" it.

"Alas," he'd cry, "it makes me pail
To think I'll kick the bucket";
And if a duck he saw for sale,
He'd offer just a duc(k)at.
Whene'er a painting made him weep,
A hue-and-cry he'd call it.
He'd curse baseball in tones so deep
That the curse—well, he'd bass-bawl it.

A schooner's mast he deemed all right,
But the captain must be master.
He never mustered courage quite
To wear a mustard plaster.
A comet left him comatose
If e'er he dared to scan it;
And the heavenly chart made him morose.
Because he couldn't plan-it.

To garden tools he'd cry "Yeo-hoe,"
An observation rakish;
And when he'd read what wasn't so,
He'd say, "Well, faix, it's fakish."
"Men should not darkly frown," thought
he,
"No matter who their frows are;
And he deemed it pantalunacy
To call a pant a trouser.

At last the worst came to the worst.
This youth so ready witted
Acquired a fit of coughing first,
His coffin then was fitted.
The marble cutter asked in doubt:
"For whom's this stone intended?"
"Why, I'm the mon-u-ment," cried out
The youth—then all was ended.

LA VIE PARISIENNE.

I am a zhentelman Francais,
  In Paris bred and born.
All foreign vays and mannaires I
  Regard viz hate and scorn.
My brozzaire Frenchmen vill unite
  In von super-r-be Amen
Ven I declare zat nozzing beats
  La vie Parisienne.

In Paris every von puts on
  Ze clothes so fine—Ah, Dieu!
Zose ozzaire nations nozzing know
  Of vot ze clothes can do.
Who spiks of taste in ozzaire lands?
  Pardieu! zat's—what you call?—
Oh, yes—cold cheek—for, as to taste,
  Dear Paris has eet all.

Ve Frenchmen are ze poets true;
  In fancy ve excel;
Ve love ze paints, ze bric-a-brac,
  Ze flowers so sveet to smell.
Ve love ze women and ze vine,
  Ze music and ze dance—
One cannot tell what living means
  Unless he's lived in France.

Ve are ze cooks par excellence,
  Our deeshes—sacre bleu!
It takes a zhenius heaven-born
  To make a French menu.
Ze epicure whose palate's cloyed
  In climates far away,
Need only come to Paris and
  He'll eat ze livelong day.

Ve have ze only journalists,
  Ze only Zola books,
Ze greatest can-can dancers and
Ze lightest-fingered crooks.
Ve are "sans peur et sans reproche,"
  All knights like Bayard still;
But, entre nous, vene'er ve fight
  Ve do not fight to kill.

Vy did I come to Amerique
  If France I love so dear?
Ah, zat's ze puzzling question, yet
  Ze answer's very clear.
You zee, I am of noble blood
  And honorable life.
But, mille tonnerres!—I'm poor as Job;
  I vant a Yankee vife.

Ze lady must have lots of cash,
  Zat's all vot I exact
And she can have my title ven
  She does ze nuptial act.
Zen back to France I'll take her, and
  I'll hasten once again
To laveesh all my vealth upon
  La vie Parisienne.

101

AT HOMESTEAD.

Golden months ago in a mill beside a
    stream
An artisan was laboring with happiness
    supreme;
The tariff hovered over him like guardian
    angels' wings,
But now another chap is there, and this is
    what he sings:

Refrain.

Do not forget me, do not forget me,
Sometimes think of me still.
    I'm from another state,
    And I don't "amalgamate";
I'm the non-union man in the mill.
Do not forget me, do not forget me,
    I'm the non-union man,
    The man in the mill.

Where are now the wages that were paid
    long, long ago?
Have they followed the example of last
    winter's ice and snow?
The scale is topsy-turvy; labor's out upon
    a foul,
And it's hard upon the nerves to hear that
    sentimental howl:

      Ref.—Do not forget me, etc.

What's wrong with Brother Pinkerton?
    Why does he weep and wail?
What cares that man of Winchesters
    about the labor scale?
Alas! his memory is keen—he does not
    like to hear
The echo of those words that break upon
    his list'ning ear:

      Ref.—Do not forget me, etc.

O fate, what is thy program now? Is it
    thy sov'reign will
To make the hapless artisan pay all that
    Little Bill;
Or is the Tide to take a turn and ter-
    minate the reign
Of the gentleman who warbles the monot-
    onous refrain:

      Ref.—Do not forget me, etc.

Cheer up, O ye who mourn the loss of
    jobs with heavy pay,
The silver lining of the cloud will yet
    come forth to stay;
And the mill beside the streamlet will with
    gladsome voices ring
When no one has occasion any more the
    strain to sing:

      Ref.—Do not forget me, etc.

BRIGGS AT THE BAR.

He did it, yes, he did it,
  And guilty he's been found.
No longer from the pulpit
  Deep dogmas he'll expound.
The deed that Briggs committed
  Is mystic, veiled and grim,
But anyhow he did it,
  And that's the end of him.

Briggs was a great professor,
  Theology he taught;
But all his skill and learning
  Have come at last to naught.
He cared not for his prestige,
  But through some idle whim
He went—ha,ha!--and did it,
  And that's the end of him.

Men fell upon his bosom
  And begged him to retract.
Fair women thronged about him
  And did the tearful act.
His brethren rallied round him,
  And plead his cause with vim,
But still, you see, he did it,
  And that's the end of him.

Accomplices he had not;
  He sought not sordid pelf,
But went ahead free gratis
  To criminate himself.
Then stood before his judges,
  Long-visaged chaps and prim.
They settled that he did it,
  And that's the end of him.

If Briggs had only chosen
  To take another path;
If in the ways of darkness
  He had not cut a swath,
He'd still be great and honored
  And in the best of trim;
But then, you know, he did it,
  And that's the end of him.

What did he do? Confound it,
  How can a layman tell?
'Twas something very horrid,
  Without a parallel.
The church's cup of sorrow
  Is filled up to the brim,
Because he went and did it,
  And that's the end of him.

105

OUIDA.

When you are in a lovesick mood
  And thrill with fiery passion;
When agonies themselves obtrude
  Because you've got a mash on.
Then is the time, when at the feet
  Of Love your spirit grovels,
To turn on lots of extra heat
  By reading Ouida's novels.

The plot—she only has the one—
  Is simple but enticing;
Nine parts there are of naughty fun
  To one of legal splicing.
Sobs, oaths, blood, tears, Italian pray'rs
  And classical quotations
Make up the giddy wheat and tares
  Of Ouida's lucubrations.

Her hero is an English lord,
  A haughty young Apollo;
Who only has to say the word
  And all the world must follow.
He versifies and plays and sings,
  Talks all the tongues of Babel,
Yet calls his talents silly things—
  This chap in Ouida's fable.

In strength he is a Hercules
  And carries all before him;
In battle bullets on the breeze
  Go whistling, harmless, o'er him.
He rows, he boxes, drinks old wine
  Along with friends from college,
Yet thinks it tiresome to combine
  All kinds of human knowledge.

Away in foreign lands he meets
  A maiden fair but lowly;
Of purest love he tastes the sweets
  And swears devotion holy.
But marriage as a gen'ral thing
  His Highness isn't much on
And so, he claims; a wedding ring
  Would "bust" his old escutcheon.

At this the maiden takes a fit
  So much the freeze-out grieves her;
The Duke don't like her plaints a bit;
  He packs his grip and leaves her.
Then, then, for sixteen thousand miles
  Or more the maiden rambles;
While he enjoys rich ladies' smiles
  Drinks deep and even gambles.

At last she runs him down and though
  He sees her not—poor girlie,
In secret gazes on her beau,
  And sheds some tear-drops pearly.
Then with an agonizing sigh
  And feeble limbs that quiver,
She ruins all her clothing dry
  By taking to the river.

The Duke, when he finds out her fate,
  Says something wise in Latin,
And straightway weds some female great
  Attired in silk and satin.
Here having made us taste the cup
  Of love's most bitter rumpus,
Miss Ouida winds her novel up
  And leaves us quite non compos.

THE CHRYSANTHEMUM.

The flow'rs of summertime are dead,
Killed by the frost and in their stead
 In gallant state has come,
Prepared to have his royal fling,
The many-hued autumnal king,
 Yclept Chrysanthemum.

What cares he for the bitter blast
And skies with darkness overcast?
 No tender chap is he;
But grows and thrives with careless grace,
His blossoms opening up apace,
 A charming sight to see.

No niggard thought his soul can sway;
He blooms and blooms and blooms away,
 Loading his branches down
With gems "of purest ray serene,"
Fit to display their brilliant sheen
 In any monarch's crown.

Anon he flashes up to view
Great blooms of golden-yellow hue
    Delightful to the eye;
Anon his fancy takes a flight
In masterstrokes of dazzling white
    That rivalry defy.

Here red and yellow he combines,
And there in Tyrian purple shines,
    Both suit him to a dot;
To dissipate at times he seeks,
And perpetrates wine-colored freaks,
    Yet call him not a sot.

Nay, for despite his football head
And dudish bang, he's gently bred,
    His ancestry's lum-tum;
He dates back to the days when man
First set his foot in old Japan,
    This proud chrysanthemum.

Unto Jack Frost we humbly pray
For grace. Deal gently with him, J.,
    This floral monarch spare;
Nor bear him malice just because
He sports that pettiest of flaws—
    A Rugby head of hair.

109

DANCING IN THE BARN.

O, 'twas down at the Bakerstown picnic,
　　Where the lads and lasses met to
　　　　dance and sing,
　　　　　　Horns a-blowing,
　　　　　　Feet a-going,
　　And a-dancing of the Highland fling.
　　　　　　(Ta-ra-rum.)
Young David, a pulpiteer prospective,
　　For theology not caring then a darn,
　　　　　　Took to skipping,
　　　　　　Lightly tripping
　　And dancing in the barn.

REFRAIN :

As he moved so gracefully (tra la-la-la-la;
　　tra la-la-la-la;)
He forgot his theology (tra la-la; tra la-
　　la; tra la-la; ta-ra-rum.)
And they swung their partners all to-
　　gether.
　　　'Twas David's opportunity to "larn,"
　　　　　　Nought regretting,
　　　　　　Pirouetting
　　And dancing in the barn.

When the presbytery met to deal with
    David,
  The clerics nearly fainted with dismay.
      "How imprudent
      In a student
  Thus to act" was all they had to say.
      (Ta-ra-rum.)
Then David, like Washington, admitted
  His fault.   Quoth he, "I cannot tell a
    yarn.
      Down the middle
      To the fiddle
  I went dancing in the barn."

      Ref.:—As he moved, etc.

Then the ministers they all   wept   to-
    gether,
  A-thinking of the days when they were
    young,
      And with Mary
      Or with Sairy
  An active pair of heels had slung.
      (Ta-ra-rum.)
So they said to him: "David, you're for-
    given,"
  But we deem it right young clergymen
    to warn,
      That we'll frown on
      And sit down on
Wicked dancing in the barn.

      Ref.:—As he moved, etc.

OUR JUGGERNAUT.

With many a bump and jar,
  With many a bang and whack,
A lumbering, hulking traction car
  Thundered along the track;
To the helpless passer-by
  A terrible fate it brought,
And still it roared in a voice four-ply
  The song of the Juggernaut.

"Scrunch, scrunch, scrunch,"
  How easy 'tis to kill!
'Scrunch, scrunch, scrunch,"
  How easy graves to fill!
And it's clear the track or die,
  That's the lesson distinctly taught,
As the ogre roars in a voice four-ply
  The song of the Juggernaut.

The small boy at his play
  With marbles, top or kite,
Must never attempt to cross the way
  With traction cars in sight.
If ever he breaks the rule,
  In a death-trap he'll be caught,
While the monster shouts, like a hideous
    ghoul,
  The song of the Juggernaut.

"Grind, grind, grind,"
  'Tis only a helpless child,
"Grind, grind, grind,"
  Though mothers with grief are wild.
What's the odds if some are slain?
  Who cares if ruin is wrought?
While the monster howls in a harrowing
    strain
  The song of the Juggernaut.

There's law to say him nay,
  There's law to bid him halt,
But he takes the law in his own sweet
    way,
  With a liberal grain of salt,
For he's backed by wealth and pow'r,
  And in vain is justice sought,
When the monster screams in accents
    sour
  The song of the Juggernaut.

"Crush, crush, crush,"
  With never a thought humane,
"Crush, crush, crush,"
  Is there any one dares complain?
"Hands off!" the magnates cry,
  "The privilege we have bought
Of bellowing forth in a voice four-ply
  The song of the Juggernaut."

MOTHER'S MUSTARD PLASTERS.

Tell us not of patent remedies to cure a
    heavy cold,
  They are mock'ries and delusions every
    one.
Dr. Quack may swear his pectoral is worth
    its weight in gold,
  And his liniment the finest 'neath the
    sun.
Dr. Do-'em-Up may brag about the syrup
    he compounds,
  While his neighbor lauds the oleo of St.
    Jake;
But there's none of 'em can drive
    away the halo that surrounds
  The mustard plasters mother used to
  . make.

Chorus.

  Who could help but to regret her?
  Who could venture to forget her?
She did honor to her sex and no mistake.
  There is joy our souls in linking
  To the olden times when thinking
Of the mustard plasters mother used to
  make.

When an infant in the winter time went
    riding on a sled,
  And baptized itself completely in the
    snow—
If they brought it home non compos, did
    dear mother lose her head
  And employ a dozen medicos?—Oh, no.
She would simply slap a mustard-pie upon
    the victim's chest,
  Steaming hot, and soon the cold would
    have to break—
Oh, 'twould take a salamander to endure
    beneath his vest
  The mustard plasters mother used to
    make.

Cho.—Who could help but to regret her?
  etc.

When the dreary thawing weather laid the
    old man on his back,
  With the rheumatiz, pneumonia and ca-
    tarrh,
The old lady used devotedly to keep him
    on the track
  Toward recovery—she was his guiding
    star.
Doctors never were admitted, for 'twas
    certain, if they were,
  That there soon would be a corpselet and
    a wake,
And in consequence the patient felt it
    proper to prefer
  The mustard plasters mother used to
    make.

Cho.—Who could help but to regret her?
  etc.

Ev'ry ailment fell before 'em; they were
    always apropos.
  Cancer, measles, typhus, smallpox—
    what you will—
Had to knuckle to those plasters in the
    days of long ago—
  There's no doubt of it but what they
    filled the bill.
Not such namby-pamby make-believes as
    those we have to-day,
  But the sort of thing to make a fellow
    quake,
Were those big volcanic flapjacks, which
    would burn and burn away—
  The mustard plasters mother used to
    make.

Cho.—Who could help but to regret her?
  etc.
115

Ah, what boots it to be weeping o'er those
    landmarks of the past!
  Times have changed and ancient customs
    are forgot;
And 'tis not the proper thing to ask for
    plasters that'll plast,
  Such affairs are classed as antiquated
    rot.
Still the mem'ry lingers with us and is
    cherished all the time—
  'Tis a heritage too precious to forsake—
Of those triumphs of the healing art, com-
    bustively sublime,
  The mustard plasters mother used to
    make.

Cho.—Who could help but to regret her?
    etc.